A Girl's Guide to Puckering Up

ERIN ELISABETH CONLEY

First published in 2009 by
Zest Books, an imprint of Orange Avenue Publishing
35 Stillman Street, Suite 121, San Francisco, CA 94107
www.zestbooks.net

Created and produced by Zest Books, San Francisco, CA
© 2009 by Orange Avenue Publishing LLC
Illustrations © 2007 by Kristin Bowler

Text set in Neutra Text; title and accent text set in Canterbury Old Style Swash

Library of Congress Control Number: 2009933015
ISBN-13: 978-0-9819733-0-2
ISBN-10: 0-9819733-0-2

CREDITS
EDITORIAL DIRECTOR/BOOK EDITOR: Karen Macklin
CREATIVE DIRECTOR: Hallie Warshaw
WRITER: Erin Elisabeth Conley
EDITOR: Karen Macklin
ILLUSTRATOR: Kristin Bowler
GRAPHIC DESIGNER: Natalie Sousa
PRODUCTION ARTIST: Cari McLaughlin
TEEN ADVISOR: Diana Kozlova

Printed in China.
First printing, 2009
10 9 8 7 6 5 4 3 2 1

*Every effort has been made to ensure that the information presented is accurate. Readers are
strongly advised to read product labels, follow manufacturers' instructions, and heed warnings.
The publisher disclaims any liability for injuries, losses, untoward results, or any other damages
that may result from the use of the information in this book.*

Kiss

Kisses are a better fate

Aside from feeling an inexplicable urge to do it, nobody really stops to think about it: that all-important, amazing act of life known as "kissing." It's something that almost every living human is dying to do. The more we talk, think, and wonder about it, the more we simply want to lock lips ourselves — but, what exactly is the fuss about?

Like love, kissing is both clear and complicated, straight-forward and loopy. It's an instinct, a desire, and an impulse. It's also a gesture, a token, and a gift. A kiss is comprised of too many things to express and is also a way of expressing so many things. A kiss can send you over the moon or crashing back down to earth. A first kiss can ignite an entire planet of hope. A last kiss can haunt you for months.

than wisdom. —e.e. cummings

Maybe no one pauses very long to ponder *why* we kiss
because we're all too busy doing it — or, at least, wishing we
were. Although we never stop to *think* about kissing, we also
can't stop thinking . . . about kissing.

Kiss cracks the mystery of lip smacking wide open.
In this book, you'll read about what a kiss means in another
culture, how to judge when he's making a move, and how to
avoid the kiss of death. You'll learn about setting the right
romantic mood and see why it's best not to be bitter when
your lips are lonely. You'll also hear what other real-life teens
have to say about their own adventures in smooching.

And along the way, you just might be inspired to go out and
snatch a nice big juicy one yourself. Because that's really what
it's all about, isn't it?

5

Table of Contents

2. The Agony, the Ecstasy:

3. Completely Kissable:

4. The Kiss-Off:
Curbing the Creeps

5. Beyond First Base:

Crazy for Kissing:

A General Look at Lip Smacking

What's All the Fuss?

There's little arguing that we are kissing fools. From movies and books to music and advertisements, the images that surround us in pop culture are constant reminders that we're dying for a smooch. You know those cuddly kissing stuffed bears sold each and every Valentine's Day? The ones forced into an eternal sugary (and literal) lip-lock by the magic of magnets? People buy those. Lots of them. And why? Everyone's obsessed with kissing.

Studies say that the average person living in modern Western culture will spend a substantial chunk — an estimated 20,160 minutes — of their lifetime in a lip-lock. It appears to be a universal phenomenon. But did you ever stop to wonder why we feel such an irresistible pull (and sometimes a deeply desperate desire) to plant one on that certain somebody? If you really think about it, kissing is kind of . . . disgusting. It's basically the act of mashing face, shoving tongue, and sharing spit.

But, despite the act's germy reality, anthropologists report that 90 percent of people on the planet engage in lip smacking. This doesn't just mean making out. There are hello, good-bye, and goodnight kisses. I thank, love, want, need, and forgive-you kisses. There are family, friend, lover, nice-to-meet-you, and feel-better kisses. There are all kinds of kisses — from pet to air, stolen to stuffed-animal. You can get a kiss anywhere — on your cheek, a toe, or the tip of your nose. The possibilities are endless.

Most studies conclude that we've been kissing for thousands of years. (No wonder lip balm is so popular!) Some philematologists (people who study the art/science of kissing) believe that kissing is a learned behavior that's been passed down from generation to generation, like saying "God bless you" when someone sneezes. They propose that the practice evolved from how cave moms used to chew up their food and pass it to their babies, mouth to mouth, like a mother bird feeding her chicks before they are able to chew on their own. Other researchers say that cave men and women used kissing to assess the compatibility of a potential partner by way of breath-smelling (hey, we *still* do that, don't we?).

Still others believe that kissing is, and always has been, purely biological—and that we're not alone in the animal kingdom with our smooching instincts. In fact, bonobo apes seem to do it (like we do) for all kinds of reasons—to say hello, good-bye, and even make up after a fight.

The scientific community can't pinpoint the origins of the kiss, but no one is predicting its demise either. The kiss, for all of its oddities and mystery, is sure to be around for a good, juicy long time.

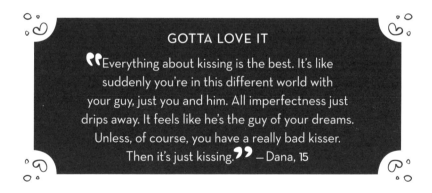

GOTTA LOVE IT

❝Everything about kissing is the best. It's like suddenly you're in this different world with your guy, just you and him. All imperfectness just drips away. It feels like he's the guy of your dreams. Unless, of course, you have a really bad kisser. Then it's just kissing.❞ — Dana, 15

In Other Words

Knowing every word there is for kissing probably won't help you with your SAT prep, but there's still no harm in expanding your vocabulary. And besides, it's much more satisfying to say that you spied so-'n'-so "sucking face" behind the gym with her BFF's boyfriend, than to simply say you saw them (yawn) "kissing."

Canoodling

Face mashing

Frenching

Giving sugar

Going at it

Gum massaging

Hooking up

Laying one on

Lip cuddling

Lip waxing

Lips, camera, action!

Locking lips

Macking

Making out

Mashing

Mouth mopping

Mouth-to-mouth mambo

Necking

Nookie

Pecking

Puckering up

Pulling

Smacking

Smashing face

Smooching

Snogging

Spit-shining

Suckathon

Sucking face

Suckling

Swapping spit

Teeth cleaning

Throat digging

Tongue tango

Tongue wrestling

Tonguing

Tonsil hockey

Tonsil polishing
Tonsil tennis
Tonsil tickling
Whistle wetting
xx (kiss, kiss)

The Culture of Kiss

"You must remember this, a kiss is just a kiss..."

Sound familiar? That lyric is from the famous tune "As Time Goes By," which was sung in one of the most romantic movies of all time, *Casablanca*. But when is a kiss really "just a kiss"? Kisses are way more complicated than that. What's socially acceptable and practiced in the world of kissing—like food, fashion, and language—varies from culture to culture.

In parts of Europe, Latin America, the Middle East, and Africa, people kiss friends and acquaintances of the opposite (and often same) sex on the cheek, rather than shake hands or hug, to say hello and good-bye. In some countries, like Argentina, it's just once, usually on the right cheek. In others, like France, it's once on the right followed by once on the left — and in still others, like the Netherlands, it's back to the right again after the right and the left. (Needless to say, it can be tiring for your lips if you have a lot of friends.) And in some regions of Italy, men and women who are just friends greet each other with a quick kiss on the lips — like lovers do, but with one critical difference: no tongue.

In Vietnam, public displays of affection are considered impolite, and even married couples will sometimes canoodle only when they're at home. In Indonesia, you can be heavily fined or imprisoned for kissing in public. And in April 2007, American actor Richard Gere was nearly thrown in jail for publicly hugging and kissing a famous Bollywood actress, Shilpa Shetty, on the cheek at an AIDS Awareness event in New Delhi, India.

21

In some cultures, people don't actually use their lips to kiss. The Inuit (who inhabit regions of Alaska, Siberia, Greenland, and Canada) rub or touch noses and inhale each other's breath (hello mouthwash!). This kind of "Eskimo" kiss is also popular in certain Pacific Island cultures, like the Maori of New Zealand, where it's just another way to say, "Hi, how's it going?" And in the Himalayas, many don't kiss on the mouth at all because they think it is dirty, what with the saliva germ-swapping factor.

But it's not just geography that impacts the culture of kissing—the passage of time does, too. Ever shared a kiss under the mistletoe during the holidays? If you had done so several hundreds of years ago, it'd mean that you were promising to get hitched (what would your parents say?)! And in ancient China, sources tell us that people kissed only in the bedroom but not in public, where it was considered vile to do so. Today, Chinese teens have moved in the opposite direction, participating in smooching contests all over China.

Why is it important to know how people around the world use their lips? Because if you find yourself in a far-flung place and longing for a smooch, it's good to know when to lay one on a local cutie and when to keep your lips sealed. At least in public.

Lip-Synching:

20 Musical Shout-Outs to Kissing

1. "The Kiss"—The Cure

2. "Kiss Me"—Stephen "Tin Tin" Duffy
   (or Robbie Williams)

3. "Always Late With Your Kisses"—Lefty Frizzell
   (or Dwight Yoakam or Willie Nelson)

4. "Kiss Me Deadly"—Generation X

5. "Bachelor Kisses"—The Go-Betweens

6. "Steal My Kisses"—Ben Harper & the
   Innocent Criminals

7. "This Kiss"—Faith Hill

8. "Kissing Song"—Dawn Landes

9. "Lips Like Sugar"—Echo & the Bunnymen

10. "Kissing a Fool"—George Michael
(or Michael Bublé)

11. "Un Beso Llega"—Juana Molina

12. "K-I-S-S-I-N-G"—Nas

13. "Kissing in the Grass"—Of Montreal

14. "Kiss"—Prince

15. "Kisses Don't Lie"—Rihanna

16. "Wishes for Kisses"—The Rosebuds

17. "Kiss From a Rose"—Seal

18. "Kissing the Lipless"—The Shins

19. "Sweet Kisses"—Jessica Simpson

20. "Kiss Me"—Sixpence None the Richer

What's in a Kiss?

When people talk about kissing, they often describe a tingly sensation moving throughout their body, right down to their toes, and their heart skipping, flipping, or fluttering. Some even say that a real good smacker can make you cry or feel faint. While these sensations sound nice and fittingly poetic, they are not all in your head. Kisses make crazy things happen in your body.

From a biological perspective, the reality of kissing is a lot more complex than just tongue wrestling. You use at least 20 different muscles when you're going at it, all of which are working together as a team. Meanwhile, your nerves start relaying messages between your brain, your skin, and the muscles of your tongue and face. Your brain tells your body to produce hormones like oxytocin, dopamine, and serotonin. Oxytocin helps you bond with your partner. It makes you feel attached, devoted, and affectionate. Dopamine and serotonin deliver happy, warm, and fuzzy feelings. Your adrenaline starts pumping, your endorphins rush, and your heart rate increases. All of this extra excitement in your body makes it completely energized. And you wondered why kissing feels so good?

BEAUTY IS IN THE EYE OF THE PUCKERER

"Kissing is the gateway for any physical action in a relationship. You may love the way a guy kisses, or absolutely hate it. Personally, I met this guy who was incredibly hot, and one night we started making out behind our gym. The only problem was he didn't even move his mouth. It was like I was kissing a dead person. The next day I heard from his friends that he wanted to hook up with me again, and I had to say no because he couldn't kiss. The hard part was all my friends thought he was gorgeous. So in the end, kissing can make or break a relationship.**"** —Melissa, 15

Hall of Fame Kisses

Nobody wants to be a bad kisser. But what lengths would you go to just to prove your smooching savvy? Check out this list of modern-day kissing kings and queens, and think about what kind of records you'd like to set yourself.

Will You Be Mine . . . for the World's Longest Kiss?

In July 2005, an English couple sucked face for 31 hours, 30 minutes, and 30 seconds. They beat out the previous record holders, an Italian couple that lasted a measly 31 hours and 18 minutes. To set the record, each couple had to keep their lips touching at all times. Who says you need oxygen?

Love-a-Palooza

In February 2007, 6,124 couples locked lips for 10 seconds straight in the Philippines, breaking the *Guinness Book of World Records* for most couples kissing in one place.

And They Call Shakespeare Prolific . . .

At a 1990 Renaissance Fair in Minnesota, a certain kissing Casanova named Alfred Wolfram planted a wet one on 8,001 people in just eight hours. That's more than 16 people a minute!

The Power of Sssseduction

In 2006, a Malaysian snake charmer kissed the head of a pissed-off, venomous 15-foot king cobra 51 times in just over three seconds. Makes the previous charmer, who managed only 11 smackers, seem like a wus.

The Art of Kissing

Ever catch sight of a cute young couple as they stop suddenly on the street corner to steal a big wet one out of simple desire? It's a nice thing to witness. Seeing others kiss can make you feel fuzzy and even a little bit, well, turned on. If you're not the easily embarrassed type, kissing can be a beautiful thing to watch.

But, of course, it's the feelings behind a kiss that make it really beautiful—even if they aren't always so simple, welcome, or happy in and of themselves. A kiss can be born out of many things: desire, love, loneliness, spontaneity. Kissing is a symbol of raw human emotion—an emotion that we usually want *more* of.

It's no wonder that so many painters, sculptors, and photographers have tried to capture its essence. See for yourself:

Throw on a beret, head online, and check out these famous works that pay tribute to the smooch.

Search for these artworks online by typing in the artist's name and the title of the piece.

Le Baiser de L'Hôtel de Ville (The Kiss at City Hall), 1950
Black and white photograph
Robert Doisneau (photographer)
This oh-so-romantic photo of a couple kissing on a busy street is practically mandatory decor in college dorm rooms. It portrays kissing at its most classic: youthful, passionate, pure, and spontaneous.

Il Bacio (The Kiss), 1859
Oil on canvas
Francesco Hayez (painter)
Italians certainly have a flair for the romantic, and this old-school Italian painting of a clandestine kiss is no

exception. The lovers clutch soulfully at the foot of a stone stairwell, kissing one another as if they might never get the chance again.

The Kiss, 1907–08
Oil on canvas
Gustav Klimt (painter)
In this classic, a couple is positioned on a dazzling gold backdrop, nuzzled together in an amorous squeeze. They cling to each other atop a bed of flowers and wrapped up in an elaborate gold quilt — and the heat of their kiss.

The Kiss, 1897
Oil on canvas
Edvard Munch (painter)
A couple cloaked in the shadows of a dark apartment share a hungry kiss, seeming like they want to devour each other. Their faces blur and blend into one. It is only

through a small gap in the heavily curtained windows behind them and to their left that one can see there is life — and a sunny day — outside.

The Kiss, 1889
Marble
Auguste Rodin (sculptor)
A naked pair sits on a marble rock with their limbs entwined in a lustful embrace. If you ever get a chance to go to Paris and view them in person at the Musée Rodin, look closely: You will see that their lips do not actually touch. Instead, they have been cast together permanently in stone — always just about to kiss.

Arc, 1990
Color photograph
William Wegman (photographer)
Two Weimaraners rubbing snouts. What's better than puppy love?

The Agony, the Ecstasy:

The Long Wait
for a Kiss

Never Been Kissed

No one talks about it, but lots of girls remain smooch virgins throughout high school. If you are one of them, you can be sure that your first kiss *is* going to happen—probably when you least expect it. In the meantime, you may feel an uncomfy mix of dread and anxiety. So much so that, at times, the idea of shipping yourself off to a nunnery seems appealing. Don't panic. It's pretty much standard human operating procedure to be majorly racked about a big event before it happens, and with a whole lifetime of anticipation surrounding your first kiss, it's a wonder you don't implode upon that initial lip-to-lip contact. (But you don't.)

If basic rationalizing is not enough to totally erase your anxiety, there are ways to at least ease it. Here are a few helpful hints on how to buck up before you pucker up.

1. **Stay busy.** Learn the banjo, play *DDR*, organize your junk drawer, join the soccer team, count ceiling tiles. Do *something* to derail the loop in your brain about what it will be like, who it'll be with, where it'll happen, how soon it is coming, and so on and so on and so on . . .

2. **Know that you're kissable.** If your time hasn't come yet, it will. So you might as well just relax that pucker until it does.

3. **Think how relieved you'll feel once it's happened.**
   This is kind of like finally peeing after you've held it for
   way too long, only better. You can also look forward
   to having something to tell all your friends . . .
   in graphic detail.

4. **Chuck expectations.** Almost
   every first kiss is awkward. That's
   part of the charm. You're not *supposed* to know exactly what you're
   doing.
   Consider your first kiss a test-run
   rather than a test that you will pass
   or fail. Consider it practice for the
   thousands of future kisses coming
   your way.

5. **Remember that just because it's a first doesn't mean it's a last.** Even if your tongue gets tied and you fumble, you'll get another (and another and another) chance to perfect your skills — probably with the very same person, probably very soon, maybe even the very same day.

6. **Don't worry about being judged.** Chances are the other person is too busy thinking, wondering, and worrying about their performance to be critiquing yours. You're both probably just psyched to be kissing, period.

KISS ME FOR WHO I AM

" I am in no rush for my first kiss. Many nights, I fall asleep dreaming of who my first kiss will be with, where it will be, and what will happen. Personally, even though I am in eighth grade, I am still not ready to kiss yet. I am waiting for a guy that is interested in my personality more than my looks and boob size. **"** —Alyssa, 14

Your Dream Kiss

Ancient secret: If you wish them, kisses will come. It's fun to believe so at least, and it's even more fun to conjure up kisses however you can. In fact, a lot of people believe there's something to be said about *imagining* what you want — visualizing the details of the moment and feeling not only like it's *going* to happen but that it already has. Some people call it scripting; some people call it the Law of Attraction; some people call it bull crap.

Call it what you will, but it's worth a shot when you're just sitting around anyway, hoping and moping. There's actually nothing newfangled or hippie-dippy about this type of creative visualization. Aspiring athletes, actors, rock stars, and politicians have used it to encourage success in their lives for years. Maria Sharipova might picture herself standing on the Wimbledon green on a windy afternoon, holding the winner's cup. An *American Idol* contender might imagine Simon Cowell dishing out compliments as she takes a bow. Think about it: When you know exactly what you want, you are more likely to get it. (Same goes for not getting what you don't want.)

So hop in a giant beanbag (or someplace comfy) and for a quiet second reflect on how you'd like your next kiss (whether it's your first ever or just first with a new love) to go down. Be thoughtful. Be serious. Be specific. Filling out the chart on the next page should help you get started.

My ideal kiss would be . . .

With:_____

Where:_____

When:_____

Thinking:_____

Feeling:_____

Wearing:_____

Hearing:_____

Smelling:_____

Tasting:_____

Touching:_____

Realizing:_____

Wishing:_____

Of course, it's always good to welcome the unexpected and to keep an open mind. There's a very good chance the kiss you've been waiting for will be even better than you could ever dream. There's also a chance that it'll be awkwardly rushed or unusually sloppy. And if it is, who cares anyway? That's just the nature of kissing.

FANTASY KISS

" I have always wanted my first kiss to be smooth and very relaxing. I want to be in a nice, quiet place surrounded by flowers that smell like a fresh summer day. Dimmed lights would surround a small two-person restaurant table. Slow, glistening music would flow through the misty air as wax candles burn under the millions of shining stars in the velvet sky. After a light, refreshing meal, we'd sit and talk for hours to each other about our interests. To conclude the evening, he would slowly lean into me and I'd slowly lean toward him. Our lips would gracefully touch until we both let go. **"** —Anna M., 15

Reel Sweetheart:

20 First-Kiss Flicks

1. Twilight (2008)
2. *She's the Man* (2006)
3. *Pride & Prejudice* (2005)
4. *13 Going on 30* (2004)
5. *The Notebook* (2004)
6. *Love Actually* (2003)
7. *Spider-Man* (2002)
8. *Amélie* (2001)
9. *Shrek* (2001)
10. *Never Been Kissed* (1999)

11. *My Girl* (1991)

12. *Edward Scissorhands* (1990)

13. *Cinema Paradiso* (1988)

14. *Say Anything ...* (1989)

15. *The Princess Bride* (1987)

16. *The Karate Kid* (1984)

17. *Sixteen Candles* (1984)

18. *E.T. the Extra-Terrestrial* (1982)

19. *Romeo and Juliet* (1968)

20. *The Sound of Music* (1965)

Sure Signs He's Making a Move

So, you're dying to kiss this guy. But does he want to kiss you? How are you supposed to know? The bad news is that it's tricky—even if you're already a seasoned lip smacker. Every new mate is bound to have a slightly different style of approach. There's the fumbler, the leaner-inner, the inchworm, and the heat-seeking missile, not to mention the hesitater, the out-of-the-blue smacker, and the old-fashioned *can-I-kiss-you?* type. It's all part of the agony (and ecstasy) of kissing—you can never be *completely* sure you'll be getting that kiss. But thankfully, there are some generic clues to watch for.

1. Virtual Lip-Lock
If he's staring at your mouth and lips while you're talking, he very likely wants to suck face. Either that, or you've got food in your teeth.

2. Lip Tease

He's constantly teasing you but not in a creepy or mean way. He punches your arm or leg (playfully, gently) when you say something funny, or even not so funny.

3. Inch-by-Inch

He's somehow squirmed his way to your end of the couch (or park bench), ever so slowly, over the course of the evening. And now you're just inches apart. Time to pucker up . . . or beat it, fast.

4. Tilt-a-Whirl

If he smiles at you and tilts his head to the side, he's probably about to come in for a lip landing.

Which Is Worse?

Kissing someone that tastes like rancid eggs **or** gnawing on a "cow patty"?

Getting caught making out with your BFF's crush in front of her **or** getting a giant cold sore right before a first date?

Giving your crush a massive bloody lip with your braces **or** dropping your cell phone in the toilet?

Accidentally puking in your date's mouth **or** watching your crush kiss your arch nemesis?

Desperately wanting to kiss your sister's boyfriend	or	finding out that your boyfriend desperately wants to kiss your sister?
Having the class loser brag about your regrettable macking session with him to the entire school	or	hearing your boyfriend say he just wants to be friends?
Being told you have death breath after what you thought was a nice kiss	or	severely burning your tongue while drinking hot cocoa?
Getting caught fooling around with the cute neighbor boy by your parents	or	flunking your driver's test because you spent the night before fooling around with the cute neighbor boy?
Being rejected by your dream guy after your first kiss	or	never having kissed him at all?

How Do I Love Thee?

There's something about lovin' and kissin' that provokes people to do funny things — like shout from a mountaintop, carve their initials into a tree, graffiti a bathroom wall, scribble in their notebook margins, or build a giant wooden horse and go into battle. (Helen of Troy, anyone?) It makes people want to advertise their passion. It makes people want to be heard. And what better way to pay tribute than through poetry, perhaps the most romantic of all art forms?

Whether you're still standing by for that first kiss or are simply waiting on the next, poetry is a creative way to help pass the time until it comes. Try these poetic forms the next time you're happy in love . . . or wallowing in heartbreak.

Haiku   A Japanese form of poetry, haikus are three lines, each consisting of a set number of syllables: 5-7-5.

Standard Rhyming Verse   This involves using a rhyming scheme or pattern. Start with an a-b-a-b scheme (line 1 rhymes with line 3, and line 2 with line 4). Then, if you're feeling prolific, try an a-b-a-b, c-d-c-d pattern. Or, you can always make up your own scheme instead.

Sonnet   Shakespeare's favorite for love poems, these consist of three stanzas of four lines each with a couplet at the end. The first stanza has an a-b-a-b rhyme scheme, the second c-d-c-d, and the third e-f-e-f. The poem is finished off with a couplet, two lines that rhyme with each other.

Free Verse   No rules, no rhyme — just write!

Or, you can simply choose to lie down on a sunny day (back to grass, nose to sky) and read what some other poets, like e.e. cummings or Pablo Neruda, have to say about giving sugar. Just head to a local library or bookstore and pick up an anthology of love poems. That's nice — and therapeutic.

Lifetime Kiss Log

We all want a first kiss with someone new to be tender, tingly, natural — and cinematic. If possible (cue the string section), you're wearing a long summer dress and standing on the edge of a cliff overlooking a tropical waterfall. But let's get serious. Most first kisses are anything but that. They happen in a friend's basement during a party, behind a tree in a park, or in the front seat of the car, just as you're getting out of it. Don't set yourself up for disappointment by having over-the-top expectations for that first kiss. Better just to hope he doesn't turn out to be a total doberman who practically chokes you with his tongue *and* drools on your favorite hoodie.

According to Andréa Demirjian's book *Kissing: Everything You Ever Wanted to Know About One of Life's*

Sweetest Pleasures, the average woman will kiss 79 guys before marriage. Even if you don't think you'll kiss that many people in your life, you're likely to kiss more than a handful. And that first kiss with that new person always seems to pass too quickly once it finally happens. So why not take time to create your own Lifetime Kiss Log? You can keep it throughout your whole life to remember, in detail, all the frogs — and the royal cuties — you've locked lips with.

Use the following pages to start your own Lifetime Kiss Log.

Lifetime *Kiss* Log

Just kissed: _____
insert name here

Brief description of the lucky person: _____

_____

Date and time: _____

Approximate duration: _____

Location details: _____

How it started: _____

How it ended: _____

Where it's going: _____

Highlights: _____

Awkward moment(s): _____

Sweet things said: _____

Do it again? (circle one):
Yes, please!   Um, that's a NO.

Overall kiss rating (scale of 1–10): _____

54

Lifetime *K*iss Log

Just kissed: _____
insert name here

Brief description of the lucky person: _____

_____

Date and time: _____

Approximate duration: _____

Location details: _____

How it started: _____

How it ended: _____

Where it's going: _____

Highlights: _____

Awkward moment(s): _____

Sweet things said: _____

Do it again? (circle one):
Yes, please!   Um, that's a NO.

Overall kiss rating (scale of 1–10): _____

Completely Kissable:

How to Get Your
Smooch On

Lips Like Sugar

If you want those lips to see the front lines, you're going to have to make sure they're armed and ready for battle. The softer, smoother, and more supple your smack machine, the more tempting it will be for someone to kiss. Here are a few basics for luscious lips.

Drink Me

Lips need hydration, too. Make sure to down at least eight 8-ounce glasses of water a day. Attach a water bottle to your hip if you have to.

Lick the Habit

Stop licking your lips! It's drying and damaging. (Spit contains digestive enzymes that can break down your lips' protective barrier.)

Wax Poetic

Invest in a good lip balm. Look for natural ingredients like beeswax, shea butter, or vitamin E. They're the most hydrating. Almond, jojoba, and coconut oils are also excellent. Steer clear of petroleum-based products, which can be drying and addictive.

I Screen, You Screen

Protect yourself with sunscreen (minimum SPF 15). Some lipsticks are actually made with it, or you can just buy a tube of lip protection at the drugstore. Your little puckers are extra sun-sensitive because they lack melanin, the pigment that helps shield skin from the sun.

Scrub-a-Dub

Exfoliate. There are special products you can buy for this. You can get the old-fashioned ones (that come in a stick) to buff away those dry, dead cells and encourage fresh baby ones, or opt for a more updated product that contains gentle fruit acid-based alpha- or beta-hydroxy acids. Whichever you choose, do not to overdo it. You don't want sushi lips.

In the Mood

If you're looking for insta-sizzle, you may want to take matters into your own hands. Setting the right mood can help multiply your chances for hot make-out sessions with your date or brand-new boo. It's all about ambiance. And ambiance is all about the senses. Read below to make sure you've got them all covered: sight, sound, smell, and touch. (For taste, see page 64.)

Dim the Lights   No one looks terribly kissable under the unforgiving glare of a bright, fluorescent bulb. (Think about the school bathroom, your great uncle's basement, your mom's office, or the DMV. *Not* so pretty.) Shoot for soft, warm, yellow(ish) lighting. The ideal is something in between so dim that you can't make out your date's lips and so bright that you need to shade your eyes to see.

Sniff, Sniff   Aromatherapy is an age-old love trap supposedly used by the likes of one of Egypt's most famous temptresses, Queen Cleopatra. Try lightly spritzing yourself with an alluring vanilla scent. Its sweet, welcoming odor is said to make people feel friendly — real friendly (wink, wink). Rose, patchouli, strawberry, and jasmine are also thought to make the nose tickle with delight.

Play It Cool   Obviously, listening to thrash metal is a *little* less likely to set off fireworks than an indie rock ballad, some R&B, or ambient tunes. If you want things to heat up, put on something chill.

Frisk 'Im   Don't be shy about giving the OoYD (Object of Your Desire) a playful squeeze, tapping his arm gently, holding his hand, or tickling his foot. Let him know that if he kisses you he won't get burned, even though you're hot.

Eat, Kiss, Love

Rumor has it that grubbing a candy bar is bad for your skin. But rumor *also* has it that chocolate can sweeten your kisses. In fact, it has long been believed that eating certain foods can hook you up, romantically speaking. These "magic" foods are called aphrodisiacs, a word that comes from the name of the Greek goddess of love and beauty, Aphrodite. Aphrodisiacs have been around for centuries — the ancient Romans prized a whole list of them, like oysters.

Of course, the true effectiveness of aphrodisiacs to make you more skilled at love and kissing has its skeptics — the US Food and Drug Administration might not get behind the slogan "a chocolate bar a day keeps romance blues away." But if you think it can give you a leg (or lip) up, why not chew on the possibility and try a couple of the following suggestions?

Hot Stuff

Scarf down something spicy — something that will make you sweat when you swallow it. Thai and Indian foods are good options. They are made with a variety of chili and curry sauces. Chilies contain the active chemical compound capsaicin, which stimulates nerve endings, increases your heart rate, and releases endorphins — just like a good kiss does. The hotter, the hotter!

Chocolate Kisses

Believe it or not, chocolate contains two chemicals (phenylethylamine and serotonin) that make you feel good. That sensation will show on your face and in your attitude, which makes you even more kissable.

Hi, Honey

Want your love life to be as busy as a bee? Indulge in a bit of honey. Medieval lovers were said to drink mead (a fermented drink made from honey) while on their honeymoon to "sweeten" the union, and the ancient Egyptians believed (though it's never been proven) that honey could cure sterility and impotence.

Green Goddess

An avocado contains lots of super healthy fats that, some say, will give your skin and hair an irresistible glow. Plus, there's something sensual about its smooth, squishy texture.

Schuck It

If you can stomach oysters, go for it. They're probably the most classic of all reputed aphrodisiacs. According to legend, Casanova ate 50 of these gooey delicacies for breakfast every morning. Now, that's dedication to the sport.

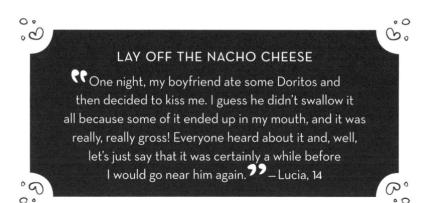

LAY OFF THE NACHO CHEESE

" One night, my boyfriend ate some Doritos and then decided to kiss me. I guess he didn't swallow it all because some of it ended up in my mouth, and it was really, really gross! Everyone heard about it and, well, let's just say that it was certainly a while before I would go near him again. **"** —Lucia, 14

Games People Play

Playing *head* games with your sweetie isn't very nice, but playing *kissing* games with your beau or with friends at a party, can be a lot of fun. If you've long outgrown the old standby, Spin the Bottle, you might want to try your luck with one of these more sophisticated alternatives.

Kiss or Dare

It's Truth or Dare with a twist. Gather the group into a circle. One person challenges another to accept a dare. If the person completes the dare, s/he moves on and chooses the next target. If the person does not complete the dare, s/he must kiss the person that laid down the proverbial gauntlet.

Ice, Ice Baby

Sit boy-girl-boy-girl (or however you please) in a circle and pass a piece of ice from one mouth to the other. The person who last has the ice before it melts wins.

Garden of Eden

Grab an apple and sit in a circle. To start, you bite the apple so that at least half is still sticking out of your mouth. The person sitting to your left takes it from you using only his mouth. If the apple falls, everyone must take one bite of it. (Try to play on a clean surface!) By the end of the game the apple will be so small that you will basically be bobbing with your tongue. If you don't have an apple, lots of other fruits will do.

Glow Worm

You'll need a glow stick to play this one. Turn off the lights and gather round in a circle. You should only be able to see the glow stick—and nothing else. One person starts off by holding the stick with her lips and passing it clockwise, to the right. Watch the glow stick disappear and notice how long it takes to reappear. Be sure not to swallow it! This is also a good time to sneak a secret smooch in the dark when the mood strikes. If you're covert, only one other person will know besides you.

Cherry Oh, Baby!

Sit in a circle. Pop a cherry in your mouth and start passing it around. If you get bored, you can always eat the cherry, spit the seed at someone, and try to tie the stem in a knot using only your tongue.

Candy Land

Gather your friends and pair off into couples. Each couple gets a wrapped piece of chewy or hard candy (Starburst, Starlight Mint, etc.). When someone shouts, "Go," each couple must try to unwrap their piece together—using only tongues, teeth, and mouths. First team to finish wins.

Secret's Out

This game is for couples. Each person thinks of a word, but doesn't tell his/her partner. Throughout the day, if one person says the other person's word that partner has to drop everything and lay a wet one on the other.

KISS ON THE COUNT OF THREE

❝A group of us went to this boy Max's house for a 'party.' We swam in the pool and then went into his basement where we put on *The Mask of Zorro* and flirted endlessly. Eventually, we ended up playing a game of truth and dare, in which we would all partner up with a person of the opposite sex and count to three and simultaneously kiss on the lips. Things started getting 'frisky' when the guys had to pick up the girls and then kiss them while cradling them in their arms. After that we went further to have the girls lie on the floor while the guys leaned over (not touching any other part of the body!) and kissed us on the count of three.❞ —Sylvia, 15

The Perfect French

Worried about your tonguing technique? Here are a few tips to help you master your mouth—and his.

👄 **Breath test.** Avoid garlic, onions, and other known breath killers. If possible, brush, floss, swish mouthwash—or at the very least pop a mint. Bad breath stinks when you're kissing.

👄 **Easy, breezy.** Smile, hold hands, touch knees, play with his hair, tickle his arm—*before* you go in for the kill, er, kiss.

👄 **Keep 'em closed.** Your eyes that is. It's less distracting, and that way you can fully focus on how it feels to be kissing.

👄 **Hold your tongue.** The French part (aka tonguing) of French kissing should progress slowly. As the kiss builds, give it more tongue.

👄 **Watch the juice.** Extra saliva production is normal while kissing, but nobody wants to mop up after a kiss.

👄 **Relax.** Pretend you're in a rowboat on a tranquil afternoon, not stuck at sea in a major squall. Move your tongue around the mouth, teeth, tongue, and lips.

👄 **Don't eat face.** A very soft nibble on the lip is sweet. But really sinking your teeth in is *not*. If you'd like to see him again, no chomping!

👄 **Oxygen!** Don't forget to breathe. Your mouth may be busy, but your nose still works.

👄 **Mean it.** Ignore the world around you. Let the kiss — and the moment — completely suck you in.

👄 **Stay aware of your partner.** Kissing is not just about your lips, it's about your love (or like) for the person you're kissing. Don't forget, the mind is a very powerful thing, and you should be consciously aware of your romantic intention while you mack down.

Smacking Styles

Sometimes it's best to just ad-lib it — to kiss without abandon in your own particular style. But other times, it's fun to mix it up and experiment with a few fresh, borrowed techniques. Either way, you're sure to *make out* like a bandit. Here are some tempting new ways to have at it.

Flutterby

With your faces touching, open and close your eyelids against your partner's. If done skillfully, the fluttering sensation will be a lot like the one in your heart. This innocent kiss is the perfect prelude to more heavy-duty lip-on-lip service.

Eskimo Kiss

Imagine the frozen tundra and cuddle close, with your

faces less than a breath apart. Look into one another's eyes and gingerly rub your noses together. Your hearts will surely melt.

Ear Pulls
Tease your partner with itty-bitty bites and a little light sucking action on the earlobe. Try to keep your kisses quiet, since loud sucking noises will spoil the mood.

Love Nibbles
Leave a little love bite (aka hickey) by either sucking or by *gently* biting the area on which you want to leave your mark. (But be forewarned: If your kissing partner reciprocates, you'll be left with a not-so-pretty love bite of your own.)

Nip Tucks
While kissing your partner, ever so gently nibble on the lips. (Be very careful not to bite

too hard!) When done correctly, this kiss can really set off sparks.

Sip 'n' Slide
Take a small sip of your favorite beverage. (Iced-cold sugary lemonade is a good choice.) Leaving a trace of sweetness on your lips, lean in and steal a kiss. It'll be a sweet surprise for the one you're sweet on.

That Sucks
Playfully suck in air from your partner's mouth while you are Frenching. This flirty gesture will take his breath away.

The Wave

A bit of practice helps with this potentially sloppy smooch. While kissing your partner, slowly roll your tongue, up and down, in a wave-like motion.

Hi-Tech Touch

Having a long-distance relationship or just miss your sweetie when you're apart? Take punctuation out of English class and send an email/text/IM kiss with a colon, a hyphen, and an asterick. :-*

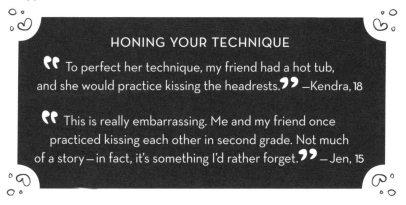

HONING YOUR TECHNIQUE

" To perfect her technique, my friend had a hot tub, and she would practice kissing the headrests." —Kendra, 18

" This is really embarrassing. Me and my friend once practiced kissing each other in second grade. Not much of a story—in fact, it's something I'd rather forget." —Jen, 15

Caught!

That hot good-night kiss on your porch with your new boyfriend can turn pretty cold when your dad shows up. Here's what some real-life girls had to say about getting caught with their mouths open.

DOUBLE TROUBLE

"I was at my friend's party, and it was pretty rowdy. I got with this guy, and we were making out on the floor when another one of my freaky guy friends got on top of the guy who I was making out with. My friends saw this and were laughing hysterically. Suddenly, we heard, 'Oh my God! What's happening in here?!' It was my friend's mom, and none of us at the party knew she was home. The guy and I flipped out. My friend who was having the party made up some excuse about how it was some dare game we were playing, and that kind of calmed her mom down. The guy and I didn't do anything else that night.**"** —Fiona, 16

BEHIND THE SCENES

"I was making out with my date, and at the end of the movie, this lady who I don't know at all came up to me and asked, 'Did you enjoy the movie?' I said yes. She then said, 'Well, I would've too if I had been kissing through the whole thing.'" —Anju, 13

THE SHOW MUST GO ON

"We were in the halls of the school while the school play was going on. My boyfriend's big part was coming up, and he decided to stop by and give me a quick kiss and then split. But he hung around and forgot he was supposed to go on. A teacher came to get him and found us there kissing." —Janey, 14

Making the Best of Bad Kisses

It's been said that kisses are candy for the soul. Occasionally, however, the candy ain't so sweet. There's an awfully unromantic side to kissing. Apart from the bigger risks of catching cold sores, viruses, and mono, kisses can also be awkward, sloppy, painful, or just plain *bad*.

If you don't actually *like* the guy, head to the Exit, Stage Left section (on page 100). If you *do* like him, here's how to somewhat gracefully deal with a few classic offenses.

That Stinks
Mints help, but those super-potent breath strips are even better. Always, always have some on hand

in case your kissing mate has a penchant for garlic fries or tuna.

Spinach Floss

There's nothing more dreadful than the realization that you've had food stuck in your teeth all night long. Except, perhaps, for the realization that he's got something stuck in *his* teeth . . . and is leaning in for a wet one. When this is the case, there are just three choices:

1. Consider it a midnight snack.

2. Silently let him know with the universal pointing gesture for you've-got-something-stuck-in-your-teeth.

3. Make a joke out of it and then, as soon as he's done digging, playfully plant one on him to let him know it's OK.

Everlasting Glob Slobber

If he's the slobbery sort, he could just be over stimulated. (That's a compliment.) Cool things down by gently pulling away mid-kiss. Hold up the just-one-minute finger with a

smile, take out a tissue, and playfully wipe his mouth dry.
You can also try stopping for a mutual sip of water.

Brace Yourself
Braces happen to the best of us. Whether he's got 'em or
you do, they can make kissing a little more complicated.
Just take care to go easy, especially with the tongue and
nibbling action. No one wants a bloody lip.

Lip Crackers
Kissing rough, chapped lips is no fun. Run his finger along
your smooth babies and then along his own, and offer him
some of your lip balm.

Raw Hide
Sure, a little 5 o'clock shadow can be sexy. But not when it
gives your sensitive skin a rash. Politely put the kibosh on
those killer kisses by pointing to your chafed cheeks and
simply saying, "Ow." If he still doesn't get it, ask him
to please shave next time.

Excuse, Me?

If he accidentally burps in your mouth, go ahead and laugh—because, come on, it is kind of funny. If he does it on *purpose*, let him know that if he pulls that again, the only thing he'll be kissing is your door as it slams shut in his face.

SLIMED

"My first kiss was disgusting! We were watching *Fast Times at Ridgemont High*. In the middle of the movie he kissed my cheek. I turned my head toward him and he started to kiss me. It was not at all what I imagined. He stuck his tongue in my mouth and moved it in a circle one way and then abruptly changed directions and moved it around the other way. There were no lips—only the slimy tongue. I never wanted to kiss a boy again." —Courtney, 16

You Want to Kiss Me Where?

20 Places to Steal a Smooch

To be honest, when you truly like someone it doesn't really matter where you are when you kiss. For those few magic moments, you might even be transported to another, much lovelier planet. Then again, there's no harm in a little romantic fantasy . . . so here are 20 of the most charming places to steal a smooch. No doubt, you and your sweetie will discover countless more.

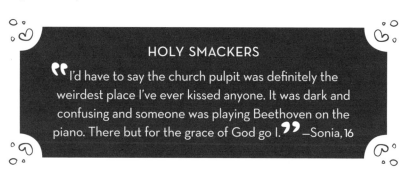

HOLY SMACKERS

❝I'd have to say the church pulpit was definitely the weirdest place I've ever kissed anyone. It was dark and confusing and someone was playing Beethoven on the piano. There but for the grace of God go I.❞ —Sonia, 16

1. Under a willow tree (no weeping!).

2. At twilight, on top of the jungle gym at your old elementary school.

3. By the sea with your bare toes dug into the sand.

4. On a moss-covered log out in the woods.

5. At the bottom of a fresh-mountain waterfall.

6. In front of the piranha exhibit at the aquarium.

7. Over an ice-cream cone (Yours: mint-chocolate chip. His: strawberry.).

8. Slumped together in a bright- green beanbag.

9. In a backyard hammock on a warm, spring day.

10. Huddled under an umbrella on a rainy afternoon.

11. On a tire swing, next to a pond.

12. In the ocean, floating on surfboards.

13. While dancing the tango or cha cha cha.

14. Right after blowing out the candles on your birthday cake.

15. Flying kites on a blustery Saturday afternoon.

16. Around the campfire, roasting marshmallows.

17. Watching monkeys swing through the canopy in the Amazon rain forest (or . . . at the local zoo).

18. On the lift, right after the last snowboard run of the day.

19. On your front stoop at the end of your very first date . . . .

20. Or on his front stoop at the beginning of your second.

DREAM KISSING SPOT

"This guy I was going out with was *super* romantic, and had a lot of secret things for me. There was this 'secret spot' that he took me to once. It was this little opening surrounded by trees that faced out to the Golden Gate Bridge. We went in the night, and it was beautiful. I had the greatest time with him, and it was super romantic. I loved it because it was so hidden from the rest of the city.**"** —Laurie, 15

The Kiss-Off:

Curbing
the Creeps

Kiss of Death Kisses

These are kisses so bad they'd be worthy of the Sucking Face Hall of Shame (if there were one). Sure, they're fun to joke about, but not so much to endure. Finally, there's a bright side for the less experienced — the fewer people you've kissed, the lower your chances of having encountered one of these.

The Washing Machine

Jams his tongue in your mouth and goes round and round at an alarming rate. Dislodges troubling popcorn kernel that's been stuck in your teeth for two hours during extended spin cycle.

Glob Slobber

Drools more than a teething baby or a dehydrated bloodhound. "Shares" so much saliva that you won't need a drink for the rest of the year.

High and Dry

Absolutely no moisture in his mouth. Tongue feels like sandpaper and white mucus foams from corners of lips.

Dog Breath

Makes you feel woozy, but not with love. Breath so bad you want to vomit.

Lip Nipper

Thinks biting your lips is cute and/or sexy, so behaves like a rabid Chihuahua. Possibility of late-night hospital visit for stitches.

Rigor Mortis

Totally stiff upper (and lower) lip. His tongue just *sits* there in your mouth. Arms hang heavy at sides. You'd get more action from a wood stump.

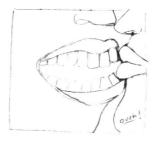

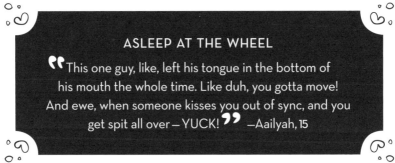

ASLEEP AT THE WHEEL

❝This one guy, like, left his tongue in the bottom of his mouth the whole time. Like duh, you gotta move! And ewe, when someone kisses you out of sync, and you get spit all over—YUCK! ❞ —Aailyah, 15

Deep Throat

Shoves his tongue down your throat as though trying to unclog a drain. Someone nearby calls 911 because of the sound of your choking.

KISS KILLER

" The worst lips I've locked with was this guy in my grade. It was horrible. He had the worst breath, therefore making that whole swallowing each other's spit thing impossible, thus leading to nasty, messy drooling. " —Jill, 16

How to Deal With a Don Juan

If you've ever come face-to-face with one of those over-confident Casanova types — the ones that feel entitled to chase after you and make a move whether you want them to or not — you know what a serious plague they can be. If you're too *polite*, you won't come close to getting your point across. If you're too *blunt*, you're an ice queen, prude, or tease — none of which is an appealing label.

So, what's a girl to do when push comes to shove? After she's tried to be decent, kind, and direct — but been burned (at the stake) for it? Here are seven little ways to lose him for good.

X Tell him you're getting back together with your ex (who's incidentally been away studying karate in Japan).

X Text him every hour on the hour until he changes his number.

X Tell him you're not into boys.

X Draw a fake tattoo with his name and face on your shoulder blade, and tell him you'd like him to do the same for you.

X Give him your "new" cell phone number. Make sure to write it down for him: 555-IT'S-OVER.

X Ask when he thinks you guys should tell his parents the good news about your engagement.

X Mash some fresh garlic into your teeth and lips, and greet him with a big stinky kiss.

Dear Scrub Letter

We've all felt the bittersweet sting of being struck by a kissing bandit. You know the type. Maybe he kissed and told. Or made out with you *and* three other girls in the very same night. Or, perhaps, he just (just?!) gave you a cold sore.

Whatever he did, he's not worthy of you or your kisses. So why not tell him exactly how you feel by writing your very own kiss-my-@ss letter? Even if you don't send it (probably better not to), it'll feel good to get it down on paper.

See the list on pages 98–99 to fill in the blanks.

Dear _____ ,
use code name for privacy

If I weren't such a cool person, I'd be tempted to

_____ **. You should know that the first time we**
choose from list A

kissed I felt _____ **, but I could see you were**
choose from list B

too _____ **to notice. It wasn't so much your**
choose from list C

breath, which reeked of _____ **, but**
choose from list D

just _____ **. Your** _____ **told me that**
choose from list E   *choose from list F*

you've been trying to hone your romantic skills

with _____ **, but that you still had a ways to go**
choose from list G

in that department. I want you to know that I'll always

be _____ **.**
choose from list H

_____
Fill in your name here

A

kick you where it hurts

put my hand over your mouth and stuff paste up your nose

tell all the other girls about your "little" problem

B

like I'd rather be swallowing fire

a little vomit come up in the back of my throat

that I could really do better

C

much of a mental moron

amazed by your terrific luck

busy trying to get your thumb out of your crack

D

butt sweat

dog poo

trash juice

knowing that I had sunk so low
everything else about you
the sight of your big dumb face so close to mine

grandmother
best friend
therapist

G
your cousin
some other poor soul
the warden at your detention center

H
truly sorry we met
out of your league
glad I got away from you when I did

Exit, Stage Left

Obviously, being straight up is the nobler way to give someone the shut down. But sometimes a quick getaway can actually be less awkward for you both. (Better than having to reject him *after* he makes his move.) So, if you sense him coming in for that goodnight kiss and are sure you don't want it, use one of these little zingers to stop him in his tracks. Then, make a run for it.

- Squeeze your legs together while rocking back and forth and say, "Sorry, nature calls."

- Look straight into his eyes, smile sweetly, and say, "I'm glad we're just friends. It keeps things uncomplicated."

- Glance at your watch and mutter, "Oh no. [*Insert TV show here*] started five minutes ago! Sorry. See you."

- Back away and mutter, "It's time for me to give Gramps a sponge bath. And take out his teeth."

DODGING A BULLET

❝I guess this guy really liked me because, at the end of the party, he leaned in to kiss me. I faked a sneeze so that he couldn't. Now that takes skill!**❞** —Lacy, 16

SMOOTH SKATER

❝This guy I ran into recently seriously tried to kiss me, and I freaked out. See, I knew him from preschool, and I didn't know he had a thing for me. I was skateboarding, and all of a sudden he grabs me from behind and tries to kiss me! First of all, I fell off the skateboard, and then I screamed because I wasn't sure who it was. Then, I like hit him over the head with the board. Hehehe! He didn't try it again!**❞** —Anna B., 15

Hickeys Are for Hiding

It probably seemed like an OK idea, when your new dude was nibbling and suckling on your neck. But in the sunlight the next day, yeah, not so much. That's when it hit: A "love bite" is really just a big ugly bruise on your neck. It's also a dead giveaway of what you've been up to. (No one actually buys the "I burned myself with my curling iron" excuse.) Next time you're necking out maybe you'll know better? In the meantime, here are a few suggestions for how to cover up and cope for the best.

HOODIE TO THE RESCUE

"A hooded sweatshirt is the least suspicious cover-up for a hickey. That way you don't have to wear a turtleneck or something, since most teens don't wear turtlenecks." —Jess, 15

Turtleneck

Beaded choker

Cute polka-dotted men's tie

Fake-tan lotion

Fluffy feather boa

Hair extensions

Hand-knitted scarf

Henna art

Hoodie

Makeup, lots of it

Pet snake

Pink pashmina wrap

Pretty, patterned silk scarf

Studded dog collar

Temporary tattoo

Turtleneck

Your hand, artfully (and permanently) placed on your neck

Down With Love:

15 Anti-Kiss Songs

1. "Shame"—Lily Allen

2. "Sleep to Dream"—Fiona Apple

3. "Irreplaceable"—Beyoncé

4. "Everyday I Love You Less and Less" —Kaiser Chiefs

5. "Since You've Been Gone"—Kelly Clarkson

6. "Walk Away"—Franz Ferdinand

7. "Love Stinks"—J. Geils Band

8. "Love Will Tear Us Apart"—Joy Division

9. "Spitting Venom"—Modest Mouse

10. "I Don't Love You"—My Chemical Romance

11. "Ruin"—The Pierces

12. "This Is Not a Love Song"—Public Image Ltd.

13. "I'm Not In Love"—The Talking Heads

14. "Everything About You"—Ugly Kid Joe

15. "Kiss Off"—Violent Femmes

PLEASE DON'T KISS ME . . . EVER

"We were at this farm with a bunch of families for the weekend. All the kids decided to sleep in the barn in sleeping bags. Michael, who I could tell liked me but who I did not like, put his sleeping bag down right next to me. Once it was dark and no one was talking anymore, he whispered, 'Can I kiss you?' to me. I was lying there stiff as a board. I pretended I was asleep. 'ZZZZZZZZZZZ.' What a nightmare.**"** —Kat, 16

Beyond First Base:

Big Decisions and Dry Spells

The "S" Word

"*Kissing—and I mean like, yummy, smacking kissing—is the most delicious, most beautiful and passionate thing that two people can do, bar none. Better than sex, hands down.*" —**Drew Barrymore**

Kissing is one thing, and sex is another. One does not (or should not) automatically lead to the other. But when things are heating up between two people it's confusing. Things can go fast. It's easy to get caught up in the moment—in the romance (seeming or real)—and be tempted to experiment with *more*. And sometimes your partner, subtly (or obviously), is urging you on.

It's good to know that it's OK to just kiss. If you don't feel comfortable going any further than that, you shouldn't feel that you have to. But whatever you do, make sure that how far you go is YOUR choice—one that you've thought about very carefully. And get informed. If you're on the verge, already engaging, or just curious about sex, there are places to turn (besides your parents, if that's a big fat NO) to get the facts you need. Confide in a trusted sibling, an older friend, a mentor, or a counselor at a local clinic like Planned Parenthood. And always protect yourself—physically and emotionally. For *that*, of course, you'll need more than a quick karate chop or a killer 1-2 punch . . . keep your head twisted on and you'll be just fine.

BASES LOADED

"One night I was with my boyfriend, and we were kissing and it just went further. I wasn't so much scared as I was excited. It went on for quite awhile, but suddenly we heard a noise and stopped. It could have gone even further, I think, but after we stopped it never started again. I'm glad about that though, because he turned out to be quite an a**, if I might say so, but that's a different story.**"** —Maria, 16

Wouldn't It Be Sweet If...

- you never had to wonder when your next kiss was coming?

- your boyfriend's cold sore wasn't contagious?

- everybody always had somebody to love?

- lipstick was free?

- your legs shaved themselves?

- only (human) rats, weasels, and players had morning breath?

- boys that dogged girls grew tails?

- you always had a date on Valentine's Day?

- you could lip-off whenever you felt like it?

- you could mentally will someone to kiss you?

- Cupid whispered the secret of love in your ear?

- you could actually delete awkward moments with the pound key on your cell?

- you could go back in time and do one kiss over?

MY SWEETEST KISS

"Outside on the sidewalk. It was raining, and he was holding me close, keeping me dry under his jacket. We looked at each other and started to kiss. It was my first kiss, and I still think of that moment, with the warm shower drizzling down as far as the eye could see, as the most romantic I have experienced.**"** —Sarah, 16

Don't Quote Me

The Internet is littered with a million gooey quotes about how *fabulous* swapping spit is. But if you aren't getting any action, you probably aren't feeling the love. When you have no game, those kinds of romantic platitudes may make you feel *something* — something like the desire to choke a clown.

But, believe it or not, there are a few words of wisdom to comfort the kissless. After reading the nuggets below, you'll see that that going a little while without isn't so sad after all. You might even be happy to hold out for the *right* kiss, rather than leave yourself ripe for the wrong one.

"*K*isses that are easily obtained are easily forgotten."
—English proverb

"*K*issing is a means of getting two people so
close together that they can't see anything wrong
with each other."
—Rene Yasenek

"A kiss is a lovely trick designed by nature to stop speech
when words become superfluous."
—Ingrid Bergman

"You have to kiss a lot of toads before you find a
handsome prince."
—American proverb

"I had a lovely evening. Unfortunately, this wasn't it."
—Groucho Marx

"Kissing is like drinking salted water:
You drink, and your thirst increases."
—Chinese proverb

"A kiss may ruin a human life."
—Oscar Wilde

"What lies lurk in kisses."
—Heinrich Heine

"Kisses are like tears, the only real ones
are the ones you can't hold back."
—Anonymous

"I wasn't kissing her, I was whispering in her mouth."
—Chico Marx

"I do not know how to kiss, or I would kiss you.
Where do the noses go?"
—Ingrid Bergman

"Perhaps when we find ourselves wanting everything, it is
because we are dangerously close to wanting nothing."
—Sylvia Plath

"Never let a fool kiss you, or a kiss fool you."
—Joey Adams

OH, YOU SAY THE
SWEETEST THINGS

"Once I was making out with a guy at the movies. I
remember I was chewing gum when we started. When we
stopped to take a break, he was chewing my gum. He said,
'Thanks for the gum, I wanted some.'**"** —Lezlie, 13

Bitter, Party of One

When your lips are lonely (along with your heart), it seems like lovebirds are snuggling *everywhere* you look. And when you're in one of those one-is-the-loneliest-number periods, it's hard not to wish you were part of a pair. It's hard not to feel irritated when you eyeball that cute couple making out in the movie theater, cuddling at the bus stop, or strolling along the pier hand-in-hand. It's natural. It's understandable. It's also the kiss of death.

Bitterness is just *not* pretty. It shows up on your face, in the clothes you choose to wear, in the words you use—even in your lunch. Sure, it's as abstract as any emotion, and yet it is not without odor, weight, or dimension. And worst of all, since it seems to be contagious, people (kissable people!) will start to avoid you . . . like the plague. So how do you shake it? How do you step out of the muck?

Accept your feelings. Let them be. And then bask in the love you *do* have in your life. Take hugs from family members and friends, let a puppy lick your face, or play hopscotch with a little kid. And next time you see a couple suctioned to each other, take a long look in their direction, and *appreciate* the love. After all, your next hot and heavy public display of affection could be just around the corner.

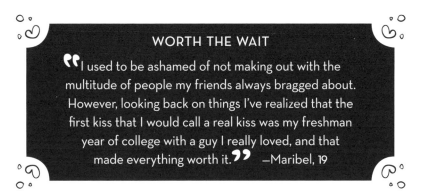

WORTH THE WAIT

"I used to be ashamed of not making out with the multitude of people my friends always bragged about. However, looking back on things I've realized that the first kiss that I would call a real kiss was my freshman year of college with a guy I really loved, and that made everything worth it.**"** —Maribel, 19

$\mathcal{P}$op $\mathcal{Q}$uiz! What Signs Are You Sending?

You may be down on your loving luck, but don't let a bad attitude keep you from making connections. If you want to appear open to potential customers, you've got to advertise by putting out the welcome mat. Take this brief quiz to find out exactly what messages you're sending.

1. **You're lunching at an outdoor café with a friend and the cute waiter serves you a complimentary Brownie Fudge Ice-Cream Explosion with a wink and a smile. You . . .**

   A. assume the free brownie is for your friend and advise her on how best to keep his attention.

   B. wonder what he's trying to say about your weight and immediately send the dessert back to the kitchen.

   C. leave him an extra-big tip plus your phone number. Give a little wink as you stroll away.

$2.$ **The captain of the soccer team (and your long-time crush) calls to ask if you'd like to come to watch him play at the big game on Friday. You . . .**

A. mutter something about homework and laundry, and fly the coop.

B. tell him you've already got plans that day — playing hard to get is the only way to see if he's willing to *work* for your affection.

C. happily accept and bring a batch of home-baked cookies for the whole team.

3. **You're working the concession stand at the movie theater when you see your dream guy approaching the counter. You . . .**

A. throw an empty bucket of popcorn over your head and hide behind the ice machine.

B. get nervous and then serve him, with a snarky smile and a half-assed attitude.

C. flash those dimples, offer him extra butter, and ask him what film he's about to see.

4. **You notice the hot Swedish exchange student — sitting alone with his nose in your favorite book — at the back of the city bus. You . . .**

A. figure he probably wants to be left alone, but you also consider learning "hello" in his native tongue for next time.

B. think about sparking a conversation about the book but decide that his English probably isn't good enough to keep up.

C. ask sweetly if the seat next to him is taken and compliment his taste in literature.

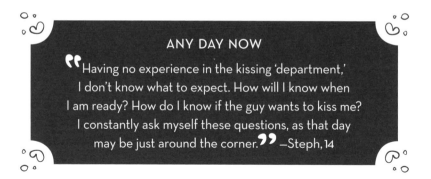

ANY DAY NOW

"Having no experience in the kissing 'department,' I don't know what to expect. How will I know when I am ready? How do I know if the guy wants to kiss me? I constantly ask myself these questions, as that day may be just around the corner." —Steph, 14

nswers: What Signs Are You Sending?

If you answered mostly As:

You are thoughtful and kind but tend to be a little on the shy side and don't always recognize your own inner (or outer) beauty. You like the idea of hooking a BF, but you need to work on boosting your self-confidence first. Take a good look in the mirror and start appreciating that lovely reflection. Once you do, you'll be a bona fide kissing bandit!

If you answered mostly Bs:

Better put on an extra-warm winter coat—cause these days you can sure be cold! Deep down you are probably a total sweetie, but you throw on a gruff exterior to protect yourself from getting hurt. Unfortunately, you're just hurting yourself in the process. Obviously, there's something genuinely kissable about you, or nobody'd even bother trying to crack your ice.

Soften your touch, and you'll find a heart-melting hunk in less time than it takes to defrost a Thanksgiving turkey.

If you answered mostly Cs:

You are a sweet, open person with a generous spirit. Generally, this openness is a beautiful trait, but sometimes you are SO open that you end up stuck with someone who takes advantage of your kindness or simply isn't right for you. With a little time and some more practice listening (and responding to!) your gut, you'll be kissing fewer toads and locking lips with that special someone soon.

They're Not Just for Kissing

So, you've hit a little kissing dry spell. Shrug it off, tough it out, and give those suckers something else to do before they petrify. And remember, it's only temporary.

Blow spit bubbles

Whistle

Perfect your bird-calling techniques

Learn to read lips

Eat a popsicle

Blow bubble gum bubbles within bubble gum bubbles

Chew on ice

Hum

Burp the alphabet

Play the bazooka

Take up the trumpet

See how far you can spit a watermelon seed

Volunteer at an old folks home and talk to the elderly

Practice silent meditation

Suck a lollipop

Yodel

New Mindset Mantras

A mantra is something you say over and over again to remind yourself of a truth that you've forgotten. It's kind of like a spoken meditation. If you're ever feeling less kissable than you'd like, try to get comfy, close your eyes, take some deep breaths, and repeat your chosen mantra. Say it aloud (or in your head) at least 10 times, or more if necessary, and you'll remember just how lucky someone else's lips would be to be locking with yours. It's best to make up your own, but in case you get stuck, here are a few suggestions to get you thinking.

♥ One kiss, two kiss, red kiss, blue kiss.

♥ Tomorrow is another day . . . for kissing.

♥ I am kissable. And huggable. And kissable.
And huggable.

♥ I am a lip-smacking magnet.

♥ The best kind of kiss is the one I won't
see coming.

About the Author

 Erin Elisabeth Conley is a writer and editor currently living in Los Angeles, California. She is the author of Zest Books' Crush, Dumped, and Uncool, and the co-author of Crap. She once clocked a boy over the head for trying to kiss her on the jungle gym. These days, she's much more open to the idea of a stolen smooch.